SECRET SANTAS

AND THE TWELVE DAYS OF CHRISTMAS GIVING

By Courtney Petruzzelli

Illustrated by Melissa B. Snyder

Secret Santas And The Twelve Days Of Christmas Giving

Copyright ©2017 by Courtney Petruzzelli
Illustrations by Melissa B. Snyder

Published by Lollipop Press
www.LollipopPress.com

Second printing

ISBN: 978-0-692-95389-1

Printed in the United States of America

To Mom and Dad,
You taught and demonstrated the self-sacrificing,
caring commitment that is Christ's unconditional love.
You put your love into action, and gave so many families the hope and promise
of Jesus through this most beautiful tradition.
This book is for you.

For Grant, Nixon, and Channing,
All that I am and all that I do is for you.
Thank you for blessing my life so abundantly.

C.R.

OFFICIAL NORTH POLE CERTIFICATE

OF

Achievement

PROUDLY PRESENTED TO

_____

IN RECOGNITION OF YOUR KINDNESS, COMPASSION, OBEDIENCE AND CHEER,
YOU'VE GONE ABOVE AND BEYOND THE NICE LIST THIS YEAR!
FOR SHOWING THE TRUE SPIRIT OF CHRISTMAS, SANTA HAS DEEMED
THAT YOU BE AWARDED A SPOT ON HIS

" SECRET SANTA TEAM "

Santa Claus
Santa Claus

You have been chosen by Santa himself,

to be a special kind of Christmas Elf.

You've heard of his list that he checks twice,

the one that shows him who's naughty and nice.

ut, did you know there's a secret one?

An exclusive list that's quite some fun!

A list that's full of girls and boys,

an elite group that Santa deploys.

e only chooses the kindest and best,

and to make his team, you must've impressed.

After watching all year through,

he has decided to pick YOU!

e's seen your kindness, compassion, and heart.

You've been in the running from the start.

Sweet child, you've been given a marvelous gift,

the ability to make the world's spirit lift.

Santa needs you to spread some cheer,

giving to someone who needs it this year.

The person you pick can be a neighbor or friend;

a teacher, a foster child, or war veteran.

On the 1st Day of Christmas

For twelve days,
you'll leave a little surprise.

Wait 'til you see the joy fill their eyes.

Santa will leave instructions for prep,

and each night you'll drop a gift at

their step.

On the
2nd Day of
Christmas

You'll run and hide so no one finds out,

it's YOU who's bringing this magic about!

Despite all their efforts to see who it was,

they'll only uncover it's gifted with love.

ou'll craft, create,

you'll wrap, and you'll bake.

It's so exciting, the difference

you'll make!

Day one, day two, day three, day four,

a blanket, some gloves, and treats galore.

Day five, day six, day seven, day eight,

hot cocoa for sipping, and fudge on a plate.

Day nine, day ten, eleven, and twelve,

candy canes, ornaments, and Santa's sleigh bells.

He can't wait to watch all the fun to be had,

and oh, what love and blessings you'll add.

It isn't about all the gifts
you receive,
it's what you can GIVE,
that's why people believe!
The joy and the hope you
will spread this season,
is what Christmas is for, the
real, true reason.

On the 12th Day
of Christmas, we
send our love to you
and pray the joy
it has given will last
the whole year through.
—Secret Santa

anta chose you for the wonder you are.

He sees that you're special and shine like a star!

 ow that you're on his
exclusive team,
forever you'll stay there and
always be!
So, Secret Santa take up your
mission,
and let's begin this magical
tradition.

If you and your family have enjoyed this book and tradition,

or it has touched your life in some way,

we would love to hear from you.

Please share your story at
feedback@secretsantateam.com
or via Social Media, using the hashtag
#SecretSantaTeam.